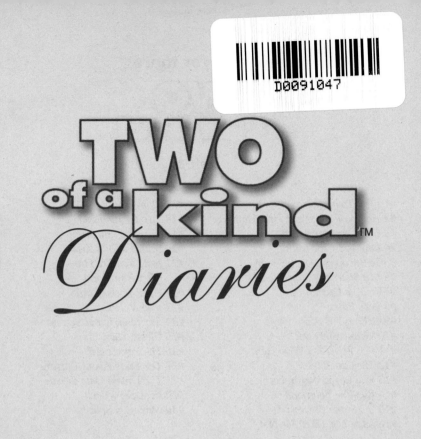

TWO of a kind™
Diaries

Look for more

TWO of a kind™

titles:

Dare to Scare

by Judy Katschke
from the series created by
Robert Griffard & Howard Adler

🎬HarperEntertainment
An Imprint of **HarperCollins***Publishers*
A PARACHUTE PRESS BOOK

A PARACHUTE PRESS BOOK

Parachute Publishing, L.L.C.
156 Fifth Avenue
Suite 302
New York, NY 10010

Published by
HarperEntertainment
An Imprint of HarperCollins*Publishers*
10 East 53rd Street, New York, NY 10022-5299

TWO OF A KIND books created and produced by
Parachute Press, L.L.C., in cooperation with Dualstar Publications,
a division of Dualstar Entertainment Group, LLC,
published by HarperEntertainment, an imprint of HarperCollins Publishers.

ISBN 0-06-009327-7

First printing: October 2003

Printed in the United States of America

Visit HarperEntertainment on the World Wide Web at
www.harpercollins.com

10 9 8 7 6 5 4 3 2 1

Chapter 1

Friday

Dear Diary,

I thought Friday would never get here. But just as the big countdown to the weekend began, our headmistress, Mrs. Pritchard, did something totally weird. She called us all to the school auditorium for a special assembly.

"Okay," I said as I slid into an empty seat in the crowded auditorium. "Anybody have a clue what this is all about?"

I glanced down the row of seats. My twin sister, Mary-Kate, sat next to me, as usual. Next to her were our friends Cheryl Miller and Elise van Hook and my roommate, Phoebe Cahill.

All of us are First Formers here at the White Oak Academy for Girls—that means seventh graders everywhere else.

"Well, I don't care," Cheryl said. Her dark brown eyes sparkled as she gave the thumbs-up sign. "As long as we get out of math!"

Cheryl was right, even though I happen to like math. But ever since Mary-Kate and I started boarding school, we've had assembly every other Tuesday. Just like we have Salisbury steak with onions for dinner every other Wednesday. And

1

banana-nut oatmeal every Thursday for breakfast!

"So what do you think, Mary-Kate?" I asked.

My sister slumped in her seat. "No idea," she muttered.

Uh-oh. It wasn't like Mary-Kate to be bummed out on a Friday afternoon. Something was up. "Why the grouch-face, Mary-Kate?" I asked.

Mary-Kate crossed her arms and slumped even lower. Finally she spilled it. "I didn't get the lead in *Our Town*!" she said. "Valerie Metcalf gets to be Emily. It just isn't fair!"

So *that* was it. Mary-Kate loves acting in all our school plays and musicals.

"You can't always get the biggest parts, Mary-Kate," Cheryl said. "Mr. Boulderblatt probably wanted to give someone else a chance."

"I know." Mary-Kate sighed. "But I told him that Emily was the only part that was right for me. So he gave the rest of the parts to everyone else."

Big mistake, I thought. *Now Mary-Kate has no role at all. No wonder she's bummed.*

"It's going to feel really weird not being in the play," Mary-Kate said. "What am I going to do all semester?"

"You can play softball!" I said, trying to cheer her up. "You love being on the softball team."

"It's almost the end of October, Ashley," sister

2

reminded me. "Softball doesn't start again until spring. That's a long time with nothing fun to do."

Elise leaned over in her seat. "Mary-Kate Cheer up, !" she said. "Halloween is less than two weeks away."

Mary-Kate sat up straight again. "Hey, I love Halloween!" she exclaimed. "Ashley, remember back in Chicago when we dressed up as that two-headed monster?"

"How can I forget?" I shuddered. "I wanted to be a ballerina. But you hid my tutu and tights."

"We did win first prize for scariest Halloween costume," Mary-Kate reminded me. "*And* best scream."

"Best scream?" Phoebe said. Her blue-framed glasses slipped as she wrinkled her nose.

"Yep. Ashley screamed big-time when she looked in the mirror!" Mary-Kate laughed. Then she leaned over and pretended to whisper: "She's kind of a chicken when it comes to scary stuff."

"Am not!" I frowned and gave Mary-Kate a nudge.

But deep inside I knew she was right.

I have to admit my sister and I are a lot alike in many ways. We both have blond hair and blue eyes.

We both have the same college-professor dad. We both have the same birthday. And we both have the same last name.

But here's where we're different: Mary-Kate likes sports and drama. I like writing, ballet, and shopping. Mary-Kate is good in history. I'm good in math . . . and shopping. Mary-Kate loves going to see scary movies. I *hate* scary movies. I'd rather go—you guessed it—shopping!

"So what's the best Halloween costume you ever wore?" Mary-Kate asked the others.

"Last year I dressed up as a hippie from the 1960s," Phoebe answered.

"But that's how you dress every day," Mary-Kate said. Phoebe's side of the closet is stuffed with clothes from antique stores and flea markets.

"Exactly!" Phoebe giggled.

Dana Woletsky turned around in the seat in front of me. She draped her charcoal-colored sweater over the back of her chair. "Try not to kick my sweater, okay, Ashley?" Dana said. "It's a hundred percent cashmere."

I rolled my eyes. As you know, Diary, Dana Woletsky is such a snob. She *thinks* she has the coolest clothes, the coolest friends, and the coolest table in the dining hall. But she's not too cool when it comes to me. We're practically enemies!

"Cashmere?" I asked Dana. "Isn't that another word for . . . *goat*?"

"If you must know," Dana said, "this isn't even my sweater. It belongs to Miranda Hong."

Miranda Hong? The rest of us all looked at one another. Miranda is sixteen—and the most popular girl in the Fifth Form!

"Why did Miranda lend *you* her sweater?" I asked.

"I guess she knows cool when she sees it," Dana said, shrugging. She flipped her long dark hair over her shoulder and turned back around in her seat.

"I don't get it," I whispered. "Why does Dana get to hang out with the most popular girl in the Fifth Form? *I* want to hang out with the older girls!"

"News flash!" Cheryl whispered back. "Dana offered to do Miranda's laundry if she could borrow the sweater."

As I was about to reply, a huge screech filled the room. It was Mrs. Pritchard, tapping the microphone. She always does that to get our attention.

"Are we ready to begin?" Mrs. Pritchard asked us. She was dressed in a dark green dress with a neat white collar. Her hair was combed in a perfect page boy as usual.

"You're probably wondering why I called you all here on a Friday afternoon," she went on. "Well, it has come to my attention that . . . that . . . " Mrs. Pritchard's voice trailed off.

A thick white fog was swirling up from the back of the stage. And a mysterious figure dressed in a long black cloak and hood was walking out from the wings.

"Oh, dear!" Mrs. Pritchard gasped.

What was going on?

A bunch of us stood up in our seats. The fog got thicker and thicker. And the hooded figure was inching closer and closer to Mrs. Pritchard!

"D-d-don't panic, girls!" Mrs. Pritchard told us. "Just stay where you are!"

"Easy for her to say," I whispered to Mary-Kate. I wanted to run for my life!

The figure's bony hands reached out for Mrs. Pritchard's neck. Gasps and shrieks filled the auditorium.

My knees were already knocking together. What was this creepy thing? And what was it doing at our school assembly?

But just as I was about to scream, the creature pulled back its hood.

"It's Miranda!" Dana squealed.

Miranda Hong tossed her long shiny hair and smiled at the audience. "I hope you all got major goose bumps!" she told us.

By now, everyone in the room was either giggling or whispering.

"Thank you, Miranda," Mrs. Pritchard said. She turned back to the microphone. "I'd like to announce that this year for Halloween, Warwick House, the Fifth Form dorm, will be turned into 'Hair-Raiser House.' It will be a type of haunted house where something spooky happens in each room."

"Cool!" Mary-Kate exclaimed.

"And it's for all the students at White Oak and Harrington to enjoy," Mrs. Pritchard added.

The Harrington School for Boys is right up the road. That's where my boyfriend, Ross Lambert, goes to school.

"The rooms will have superscary themes," Miranda spoke up. "Like gross bugs, ghosts, vampires . . . and geeky dates. Just kidding!"

"She is soooo funny!" Dana said loudly.

"A few girls from each form will be selected to help put Hair-Raiser House together," Mrs. Pritchard told us. "They'll get to work as actors, designers, and stagehands."

"Hey, you guys!" I whispered to Mary-Kate and

my friends. "Wouldn't it be great if we all got picked?"

"Dream on." Cheryl sighed. "You know Dana will do anything to make sure Miranda picks her and her snobby friends."

No doubt about that. I could already hear Dana making plans for her and her friends: "Kristen, you'll play the tormented prom queen with special powers. Brooke, you'll play the evil cheerleader!"

But deep inside, I'm feeling hopeful, Diary. I mean, how great would it be if Mary-Kate and I were *Both* picked to work on Hair-Raiser House?

Dear Diary,

You're not going to believe what just happened. Not in a million, gazillion years!

It all started about fifteen minutes ago in our dorm, Porter House. My roommate, Campbell Smith, and I were getting ready to head to the TV room to watch a baseball game. I was just pulling on my Chicago Cubs cap when I heard a knock at our door.

Campbell glanced up. "I wonder who that is," she said.

"It's probably Ashley," I said, walking toward the door. "She said she'd come with us and watch the game."

"Ashley?" Campbell asked, surprised. "I thought she didn't like baseball."

"She doesn't," I said. "She likes the baseball *players*."

I pulled open the door. No one was there. I glanced down the hall. It was empty. *That's weird*, I thought.

I was about to step out when I saw a pizza box lying on the floor. "Campbell, did you order a pizza?" I asked as I picked up the box.

"No," Campbell said. She looked confused, too. "Pizza night is Tuesdays, not Fridays."

I carried the warm box into our room and placed it on my desk. It smelled yummy. I pulled open the lid. "Hey, check this out!" I said. "There's a message written on the pie. With green olives and peppers!"

Campbell came over and read the message out loud: "'U...2...R...CHOSEN.'"

"Chosen for what?" I asked. Then I spotted something stuck to the inside of the box—a piece of paper folded in half. I ripped it off and unfolded it.

Another message.

"It says, 'Mary-Kate and Campbell, report to Warwick House *now*!'" I said.

"Warwick House?" Campbell ran her hand through her short brown hair. "As in . . . Hair-Raiser House?"

"Wow!" I gasped. "Campbell, do you think we've been picked to work on Hair-Raiser House?"

A second later, Ashley and Phoebe ran into our room. Ashley was holding a pizza box, too.

"Look what we got!" Ashley squealed. She flipped open the box to reveal the same message. But theirs was written with pepperoni and anchovies!

"We got the same message," I said, pointing to our own pizza.

"Are you thinking what I'm thinking?" Phoebe asked.

"What if we were *all* picked to work on Hair-Raiser House?" Campbell wondered out loud.

"There's only one way to find out," I said. "We have to do what the message says and go to Warwick House!"

Chapter 2

Saturday

Dear Diary,

I can't believe it. Here it is, 7:00 A.M. on a Saturday morning and I can't even sleep in late. I'm way too psyched!

Last night Ashley, Campbell, Phoebe, and I couldn't wait to find out what our pizza messages meant.

"We got a private invitation to a Fifth Form dorm!" Ashley squealed.

The fall leaves crunched under our feet as we walked toward Warwick House. It was chilly for October, so we could see our breath in the air.

"There it is!" I pointed in the distance. "Warwick House."

We stopped in front of the big brick building. I knew the bricks were red and the shutters were white. But in the dark, everything looked like different shades of gray.

"What are we waiting for?" Phoebe said. "Let's ring the bell!"

We walked toward the door but something seemed weird. The windows were completely dark. And everything inside was very, very quiet.

I didn't get it. No dorm at White Oak was that quiet—especially not on a Friday night.

"Where is everybody?" Campbell asked.

Ashley frowned. "This is creepy," she said. "Maybe we shouldn't go in."

"It's okay," I told Ashley. "Most of the Warwick girls are probably at the U. Or in town on dates."

But when I tried to ring the doorbell, it didn't work! "Must be broken," I said with a shrug.

I grabbed the big brass knocker. The handle made a loud, booming noise when I knocked.

After what seemed like forever, a girl opened the door. She was wearing a long, flowing white dress and a white veil over her face. She looked pretty creepy. "Hi," I began. "We're—"

"Walk this way!" the girl interrupted.

We looked at one another and shrugged—except for Ashley, who was still spooked. Then we followed the girl down a long hallway. We stopped in front of a closed door.

"Knock four times," the girl commanded, "and open the door slowly. Do not speak until you are spoken to. And remember . . . be scared. Be very, very scared!"

"I'm already scared!" Ashley whispered to me.

Not me. This was totally cool! I opened the door.

"Welcome!" a voice said from inside the room.

Dare to Scare

A bunch of Fifth Form girls were sitting behind a long wooden table. One of them was Miranda Hong. She was wearing a black turtleneck sweater, low-rise jeans, and big, silver hoop earrings.

Standing to one side of the room was Dana. Had she been chosen, too?

"Ashley, Mary-Kate, Phoebe, Campbell, and Dana," Miranda began. "The Planning Committee of Hair-Raiser House has chosen you five out of all the First Form to participate in this special task."

We looked at one another and gasped. It was true! We *were* chosen!

"You picked them? *Them?*" Dana asked Miranda. "But what about Kristen? She's my best friend!"

"Kristen was next on the list." Miranda shrugged. "So if one of you guys doesn't work out, Kristen will step in."

"I don't get it. Why did you pick *us*?" Phoebe asked.

"Mrs. Pritchard and some of the teachers told us to," Miranda said, "for all different reasons. We picked Campbell to set up the props, Phoebe for her design skills, Ashley to write, and Mary-Kate for her acting ability."

Yes! I punched my fist in the air. I was going to act this semester after all!

"Um, excuse me," Ashley asked the committee, "but what exactly am I going to be writing?"

Miranda smiled. "We need you to write some really creepy scenes that will be performed in the Hair-Raiser rooms," she replied.

Ashley nodded. "That sounds like fun!"

"What will I be doing?" Dana asked.

"Oh, you've got the most awesome job, Dana," Miranda told her. "You'll be playing the hunch-backed guide!"

Dana's jaw dropped. "H-h-hunchbacked? You mean I have to be . . . *ugly*?"

Miranda didn't answer. Instead she stood and walked around to our side of the table. "Don't get too excited now," she warned, "because you're not in for an easy ride."

"What do you mean?" Campbell asked.

Miranda raised a perfectly manicured finger. "You have until next Wednesday to prove you're right for the job," she said. "If you don't, we'll have to pick students from our second-choice list to take your places."

"Prove ourselves?" Ashley asked with a nervous giggle. "This sounds like some sort of initiation or something."

"It is!" Miranda declared. "And you'll begin working on Hair-Raiser House tomorrow. Ashley has to start writing, Campbell has to start setting up, and Phoebe needs to pick out costumes and props. And oh yeah. Mary-Kate has to audition."

"Audition?" I repeated. "Like I do for school plays?"

"Exactly," Miranda said. "Mary-Kate, you have to prove to me and everyone else at White Oak that you can be totally scary. Do you think you can do it?"

Was she kidding? I may not have gotten the lead in *Our Town*, but I'm a really good actress. "Sure I can!" I said.

"But what do *I* have to do?" Dana asked.

"You can keep doing my laundry," Miranda said sweetly.

She introduced us to the other committee members: Jasmine, Abby, and Stacey. Then she gave us a big cheerleader-style smile and said, "Congratulations to you all. Now get out there and prove you've got the right stuff to do the job!"

Our feet barely touched the ground as we hurried back to Porter House—that's how excited we were. Me, Ashley, Phoebe, and Campbell, anyway.

Dana walked a few feet behind us. She was probably still bummed about her friend Kristen. I was sort of surprised, too, that Miranda didn't choose them instead of us.

"See, Ashley?" I said. "I told you—there was nothing to worry about."

"Worry? Me?" Ashley said. "Ha, ha, ha."

Diary, being picked for Hair-Raiser House is the best thing that's happened to me all semester. And the news couldn't have come at a better time.

I mean, who needs *Our Town*? I'll be acting at the coolest haunted house on campus!

Valerie Metcalf—step aside!

Dear Diary,

Guess what? Last night I was cho- sen for Hair-Raiser House! That means I'm on my way to making friends with the most popular older girls in the whole school!

Here's what I mean: Today, Miranda and her friend Abby said hi to me in the dining hall! *Me!* The last time any Fifth Former spoke to me on the lunch line was to say, "Don't hog the butterscotch pudding!"

Now all I have to do is prove to Miranda and the committee that I can write superspooky scenes for

Hair-Raiser House. So today at lunch, Phoebe and I got right to work.

We started asking kids at our table what gives them goose bumps. That way, Phoebe and I could design rooms based on their worst nightmares.

Mary-Kate was all ears. She needed tons of ideas, too—on how to scare the socks off Miranda Hong and the other Warwick girls.

"Come on, Summer, give!" I urged one of our friends. "What scares you the most in the whole world?"

"Hmm." Our friend Summer Sorenson wrinkled her nose. "Getting a zit. On the night of a big dance," she said.

"A *zit*?" Mary-Kate asked. "That's your biggest fear?"

"Uh-huh," Summer said.

"Sorry." I sighed. "Zits are not the type of nightmare we're looking for."

Dana and Kristen came over with their trays and actually sat at our table. "Did someone say nightmare?" Dana asked.

I nodded. "We're thinking of scary things to do at Hair-Raiser House."

Dana looked me straight in the eye. "You don't have a clue what scary really is, Ashley," she said. "Not until you find out what the girls of Warwick

House are planning for us." She was biting her lip as she ripped her tuna sandwich into tiny little pieces. As if she was nervous about something.

"What are you talking about, Dana?" I asked.

"They're planning to scare us Hair-Raiser wanna-bes!" Dana replied.

"What's that supposed to mean?" Mary-Kate asked.

"How do you know?" Campbell asked.

Dana leaned in and whispered, "This morning I heard everything when I brought back Miranda's laundry. They're calling it 'Operation Fright Night.' And it's all part of our initiation."

Fright Night? I gulped. That did not sound good.

"What are they planning to do to us?" Phoebe asked.

Dana shook her head. "I don't know," she said. "Miranda and the others stopped talking when they saw me."

"Come on, Dana." Mary-Kate waved a hand. "How bad could it be?"

"How *bad*?" Dana asked. "Let's put it this way. Just imagine your worst nightmare!"

My worst nightmare would be to float down Lake Michigan in a rainstorm without a life pre-server. It couldn't be *that* bad, could it?

"I'm having second thoughts about this Hair-

Raiser House," Dana said with a shudder. "Maybe you all should, too. Especially Ashley."

"Why *me*?" I squeaked.

"Well, look at you, Ashley," Dana said. "You're shaking already."

"Like a smoothie in a blender!" Kristen put in.

"I am not!" I said. I gripped the edge of the table to keep from trembling.

"If you ask me, it looks like you have some serious fear issues," Dana said. "You should probably just quit before the girls of Warwick House scare you to—"

"Hey, you guys, check this out!" a voice interrupted.

I looked up. Cheryl was lugging a big striped box to our table. "Look what I got in my latest care package," she announced. "A whole box of Delightful Doughnuts!"

"Mmmmmmm," Mary-Kate said. "I love those."

My sister and I are huge Delightful Doughnuts fans. And we love Dougie, the Delightful Doughnut Boy. He's a cartoon baker with doughnut eyes and a  cherry nose. His eyebrows are made of rainbow sprinkles, and his smile is a cinnamon cruller. He's in all the Delightful Doughnut TV commercials.

"And guess what?" Cheryl said. She plopped the box on the table. "This time the doughnuts came with a free Dougie mask. Just in time for Halloween!"

I forgot all about Fright Night as Cheryl passed around the yummy dough-nuts. I chose my favorite: chocolate glazed. Phoebe and Summer went straight for the jelly doughnuts. Mary-Kate grabbed a powdery Bavarian cream. Campbell took two cinnamon crullers. But when Cheryl passed the box to Dana, she frowned.

"No thanks!" Dana said. She turned her face to the side and pushed the box away. "I hate Delightful Doughnuts."

"Who hates doughnuts?" Cheryl pulled the Dougie mask out of her backpack. She held it over her face and began to sing, "Delightful Doughnuts are so sweet! Just the thing when you need a treat—"

"I'm out of here!" Dana jumped up from her chair. "Come on, Kristen."

"Uh, sure," Kristen said. She stood up, grabbed a doughnut, and followed Dana out of the dining hall.

"What was *that* all about?" Phoebe asked.

"Dana's probably just nervous about Fright Night," Mary-Kate said. She licked powdered sugar from her lips. "Not that she has any reason to be."

I remembered what Dana had said about Fright Night. *Our worst nightmares.* If that wasn't any reason to be nervous—I don't know what is!

"Maybe Dana is right," I said slowly. "Maybe working on Hair-Raiser House *isn't* such a good idea."

"Get over it, Ashley!" Campbell said through a mouth full of cinnamon sugar. "It's going to be fun!"

"Working on Hair-Raiser House is a chance in a lifetime," Mary-Kate agreed. "Just think of all the new friends we'll make with the older girls."

"And who knows?" Phoebe said. "In a few weeks we might even get to sit at Miranda Hong's lunch table!"

I bit my lip. Then I looked over at Miranda's table. She and all her Fifth-Former friends were wearing the coolest clothes and eating veggie wraps. One girl was passing around pictures— probably of her latest boyfriend!

Miranda caught me staring. She smiled and gave me a little wave. I waved back.

"You're right," I told Mary-Kate and my friends.

"Hair-Raiser House is the chance of a lifetime."

"So you're still in?" Mary-Kate asked.

I nodded. "Sure. It won't be so bad. I guess I just have a wild imagination, that's all."

"Excellent," Phoebe said. She licked strawberry jelly from her thumb. "Then start imagining the spookiest, most bone-chilling, spine-tingling rooms for Hair-Raiser House!"

But all I could imagine for the rest of the day was something a whole lot scarier. Diary, what are the girls at Warwick House planning to do to us?

Chapter 3

Sunday

Dear Diary,

My head has been spinning all day— and *not* because I ate several doughnuts yesterday. It's already Sunday afternoon— and I still don't have a clue on how to act scary!

"Why don't you imitate some of the greatest monsters in movie history?" Jordan Marshall asked as we sat together in the Student U.

Jordan is a First Form student at the Harrington School for Boys. He is also my boyfriend.

"You mean like Frankenstein?" I asked. "Or Dracula?"

"Or the Werewolf!" Jordan said, his green eyes shining. "You can run into the dining hall with hair all over your face and hands!"

"Forget it," I told him. "I'm getting itchy just thinking about it."

Samantha Kramer and Alyssa Fuji walked over to us.

"Wow, Mary-Kate!" Alyssa exclaimed. "I always knew you were a good actress. But I never expected *this!*"

"What?" I asked.

"Duh!" Samantha said. "Do you know how many kids wanted to act at Hair-Raiser House? All my friends wanted to. And they picked you!"

"You must be so excited," Alyssa gushed.

Samantha smiled and nodded. "Congratulations, Mary-Kate!"

"Um, thanks." I stared at Alyssa and Samantha in amazement as they walked away.

"Jordan, did you hear that?" I said. "I guess acting at Hair-Raiser House is an even bigger deal than I thought."

"Gee, can I have your autograph?" Jordan joked.

The door of the U swung open, and everyone gasped. My cousin Jeremy Burke was staggering into the room— with an arrow sticking through his head! "Has anyone seen the school nurse?" Jeremy croaked as he fell on his knees. "I've got this wicked headache!"

I rolled my eyes. Just another one of my cousin's dumb jokes!

"Made ya look, made ya look!" Jeremy cried as he pulled the trick arrow off of his head. He was still laughing as he walked over to Jordan and me.

"Where did you get that thing?" Jordan asked.

"From the Gag of the Week Club!" Jeremy said

proudly. "The trick arrow came in the third kit."

"'Gag of the Week?'" I cried. "You mean you're going to do stuff like this every single *week*?"

"You bet," Jeremy said. "So far I've got a ton of fake eyeballs, scars, fangs, blood capsules, rubber hands—everything I need to scare the whole school!"

My beanbag chair crunched as I sat up straight. Did he say *scare*?

"Whoa!" I said to Jordan. "Maybe fake eyeballs and scars are just what I need to pass my audition. What do you think?"

"The grosser the better!" Jordan agreed.

"Huh?" Jeremy looked totally confused. And totally horrified when I jumped up and gave him a big hug!

"Jeremy," I said. "Did I ever tell you that you're the best cousin in the whole wide world?"

And for once in my life, I meant it!

Dear Diary,

Today we had a big Hair-Raiser production meeting at Warwick House. But while Phoebe was showing the committee her room plans, I kept wondering, *When are they going to scare us? And how?*

After the meeting, Phoebe and I headed to Porter

House. Halfway there I realized I was missing my favorite pen, the see-through one filled with water and tiny floating frogs.

"I've got to go back for it, Phoebe," I said. "I've had that pen since fifth grade."

"Okay," Phoebe said. "But make it quick. We have to plan Queen Vampira's Cave."

I ran all the way back to Warwick House with my backpack on my shoulder. Just as I was about to enter the lounge, I heard voices inside.

It was the Hair-Raiser Committee.

"Do you think they suspect anything?" Miranda was asking.

"Nope," Jasmine said. "But once they find out, it'll be a night they never forget!"

I froze. Were they talking about Hair-Raiser House . . . or Fright Night?

"I think we should send the First Former somewhere creepy," Miranda said. "Like some abandoned building with broken windows and cobwebs!"

The First Formers? I thought. *That's us!*

They *were* talking about Fright Night!

"And once they get there," Miranda went on, "it'll be totally quiet."

"And dark!" Abby added. "Let's make them all wait in the dark!"

"And when the time is right," Miranda said slowly, "we'll jump out and—"

THUD!

I jumped. My backpack had fallen off my shoulder and hit the floor!

"Who's out there?" Miranda called.

I held my breath. Very, very quietly I picked up my backpack. I decided that I didn't need my favorite pen after all. I turned and ran back to Porter House!

It's just like Dana said, Diary. The cool girls of Warwick House are planning to scare us.

And there is nothing cool about *that*!

Dear Diary,

I usually feel pretty gross on Monday mornings. But I never thought I could *look* so gross!

Thanks to Jeremy, my face and hands were covered with fake, oozy-looking scars. And stuck over one of my own eyes was a bulging rubber eyeball with spidery veins!

My cousin grinned as we stood outside the

White Oak dining hall. I could hear the kids inside clanging their breakfast dishes.

"You look totally gross!" Jeremy said. "Like ten-day-old meat!"

"Good," I said.

"Like chopped-up rhino guts with—"

"Okay, Jeremy!" I broke in. "I get the picture!"

We peeked inside the dining hall. Ashley and our friends were there. So were Miranda and the Hair-Raiser Committee.

"Perfect," I whispered. Then I saw Mrs. Pritchard at the teachers' table. "I can't do this!" I said, shutting the door. "Not with the *headmistress* watching!"

"Who says you can't?" Jeremy asked. "When the Head sees you, she'll know she picked the right girl for the job. And that's a beautiful thing."

I stared at my wacko cousin. Maybe Jeremy was right—for a change. "Okay," I said, nodding. "I'll do it."

"All right!" Jeremy cheered. He opened the door and shoved me inside. And I put my acting skills to work.

"Owwww!" I cried. I staggered through the dining hall. "Has anyone seen the school nurse?"

A few kids gasped. Some stood up.

It's working, I thought as I swayed back and forth. *In just a few seconds I'll have everybody screaming!*

I stumbled between the tables. I clawed at kids with my phony scarred hands. I knocked over a cup of juice and a pile of napkins. Soon I was standing at the teachers' table—right behind Mrs. Pritchard!

"Oh, my!" Mrs. Pritchard said.

I was about to lean over the Head's shoulder when I felt a tiny twitch under my fake eyeball. Then the bulgy rubber eye popped right off. It landed with a *splat* in Mrs. Pritchard's bowl of oatmeal!

The dining hall was silent as Mrs. Pritchard spooned the eyeball out of her oatmeal.

Suddenly I heard a giggle. Then another. And another!

Soon everyone in the dining hall was hysterical. Everyone except Miranda Hong. She just rolled her eyes.

"That was very funny, Mary-Kate!" Mrs. Pritchard chuckled.

Wait a minute! I wasn't supposed to be funny! I was supposed to be gross. Repulsive. Terrifying. *Anything* but funny!

Mrs. Pritchard wiped off the eyeball with a paper napkin and handed it back to me. "Well done!"

"Th-thank you, Mrs. Pritchard," I stammered.

I was about to bolt out of the dining hall when Miranda walked by with her tray. She looked at the fake eyeball I was holding in my hand. "Remember, Mary-Kate," she said, "you're supposed to be *scary*. Not funny."

"Yeah." I sighed. "I know."

Miranda was definitely trying to tell me something, Diary. That I was off to a *bad* start!

Chapter 4

Tuesday

Dear Diary,

One more day! That's how much time I have left to scare the whole school—and Miranda Hong. So far all I've done is pop an eyeball into a bowl of oatmeal.

"I'm doomed, Campbell," I said as we walked across campus. "I'll be booted from Hair-Raiser House for sure!"

It was the midday break. Campbell was carrying a bunch of props over to Warwick House. She had a stuffed eagle under one arm and an empty picture frame under the other. She was wearing a purple wig over her short brown hair.

"Why don't you dress up as a failing report card?" Campbell asked. "That's scary."

"Very funny," I said.

Just then Valerie Metcalf crossed in front of us. It looked like she was headed toward the White Oak theater. She glanced at me and waved. "You are so lucky, Mary-Kate," Valerie said. "I would have given anything to work on Hair-Raiser House!"

I stared at her, surprised. "Really?" I asked.

"Yeah." Valerie sighed. "But instead I'm acting in some dumb school play. See ya!"

I couldn't believe my ears. Even Valerie Metcalf wanted my part! "I *have* to stay in Hair-Raiser House, Campbell," I said. "No matter what!"

We kept on walking through the orange, red, and brown leaves. Campbell tripped on a tree root and lost her grip on the picture frame. It tumbled to the ground. Luckily it didn't break.

"Hey, there's no picture in that frame," I said as she picked it up. "How come?"

"It's for the Ghost Gallery at Hair-Raiser House," Campbell said. She held the empty frame in front of her face. "You stand behind it like this. And when people walk by, you move your eyes back and forth."

I giggled as Campbell acted it out. "You look like one of the headmistress portraits in the dining hall come to life!"

"An ex-headmistress come to life?" Campbell shook her head. "That *is* scary."

Suddenly I had a major brain click. "That's it!" I cried.

"What?" Campbell asked.

"I can pretend to be an ex-headmistress behind that empty frame," I said excitedly. "I'll move my eyes and my hands—and spook the whole dining hall!"

Campbell raised an eyebrow.

"I'll get an old-fashioned dress, a wig, and some stage makeup from the drama department," I rushed on. "And glasses to cover part of my face!"

Campbell snapped her fingers. "Hey, I know a way we can make the frame look like it's hanging on the wall with you behind it!" she said.

"How?" I asked.

"Last semester I helped dust all the portraits for Spring Cleaning Day," Campbell explained. "When I took down the portrait of Prudence Whitehead, there was this big window behind it."

"A window?" I asked. "Huh?"

Campbell nodded. "They used to use the window to pass food from the kitchen into the dining hall."

"Oh, I get it," I said, nodding. "We take down the picture of Prudence and replace it with the empty frame."

"And you stand in the kitchen behind the frame," Campbell added. "Looking just like old Prudence Whitehead."

"Only scarier," I cut in. "Campbell, you're a genius!"

"Tell that to my history teacher," Campbell said.

33

So that's the next brilliant new plan, Diary. Tomorrow morning at breakfast I'll make the whole dining hall scream.

And *not* with laughter this time!

Dear Diary,

All I can think about is Fright Night. And the horrible things I heard the other day!

"Dana wasn't making up that Fright Night stuff," I told Mary-Kate and our friends after dinner that night.

"I told you!" Dana said.

Mary-Kate, Phoebe, Campbell, and I were having our own Hair-Raiser House meeting in the Porter House lounge. Dana was there, too.

"Oh, come on!" Mary-Kate said. She cracked a grin. "How bad can it be?"

Mary-Kate was in a great mood. She and Campbell had figured out a way to freak out the whole dining hall at breakfast tomorrow.

"That's what you think," I told my sister. "They want us to go to some abandoned building. And then they're going to jump out at us and . . . and . . . "

"And what?" Campbell asked.

"I don't know," I said. "That's all I heard."

Mary-Kate and our friends glanced at one

another. I could tell they weren't buying any of this.

"Look, Ashley," Phoebe said. "Why don't you read us some of those scenes you wrote for Hair-Raiser House? That should take your mind off things."

It was worth a shot. I opened my special Hair-Raiser House notebook. "I hope the Warwick girls like what I came up with," I said. "Here's one. Queen Vampira rises from her coffin. She sees the spiders clinging to the overhanging cobwebs. She plucks one and pops it in her mouth—"

"Wait a minute, you guys," Dana interrupted. She looked straight at me. "What if the Warwick House girls drop real live spiders on our heads?"

"Ewww!" Phoebe said. "That's gross!"

"Next scene," I said quickly, turning the page. "Dr. D. Kay stands in his lab surrounded by bubbling beakers. He grabs one and begins to drink—"

"Oh, no!" Dana cried. "What if they make us drink something really disgusting!"

"You think they'd do that?" Campbell asked.

Dana shuddered. "And that dark room they were talking about," she said. "It might even be filled with—bats!"

"B-b-bats?" I cried. This was getting worse and worse!

Dana patted my shoulder gently. "It's okay, Ashley," she said. "You don't have to go through with this."

Was she kidding? Of course I had to go through with this! How else would I ever get to sit at the Fifth Formers' lunch table?

On the other hand, what if I didn't survive Fright Night? Then it wouldn't even matter.

I jumped up from my chair. "Gotta go!" I cried. "I have to study for a math test tomorrow!"

"But I'm in your math class, too, Ashley," Phoebe said, confused. "We're not having a test."

"We will someday!" I grabbed my notebook and bolted out of the lounge.

Dana was right about Fright Night, Diary. And she's probably right about something else.

Maybe I *should* quit Hair-Raiser House—before it's too late!

Chapter 5

Wednesday

Dear Diary,

This morning it was all systems go! Campbell had talked the hairnet ladies into letting us into the dining hall half an hour before breakfast. That gave me plenty of time to put on my Prudence Whitehead costume. It also gave Campbell plenty of time to set up the trick picture frame!

"This *has* to work, Campbell," I said as I took my place in the old kitchen behind the window. "Today is Wednesday. It's the last day I get to prove myself."

"It will work," Campbell insisted. She held up the real portrait of Prudence Whitehead. "See? You look just like old Prudence herself!"

"Thanks to the theater department," I said.

I was wearing a high-collared dark dress, a gray wig, tiny gold-framed eyeglasses, and lots of pasty-white powder on my face. In my hands was an old, leather-bound book.

"So how does it feel to be a headmistress?" Campbell asked.

"This wig really itches," I

37

complained. "And every time I breathe, this stinky face powder makes me want to sneeze."

I could hear voices and footsteps outside the big double doors. Everyone was arriving for breakfast.

"Quick!" Campbell said. "Strike a pose!"

"Okay!" I whispered. I clutched the book against my chest. And cracked a tiny headmistress-smile.

The doors swung open. Campbell slipped into the breakfast line as girls started filing into the dining room. I tried darting my eyes as a few of them passed my portrait.

"Darcy?" A girl nudged her friend. "Did that portrait just . . . move?"

I stared straight ahead, perfectly still.

"Move?" Darcy laughed. "Jenny, all that studying is beginning to fry your brain!"

More kids walked by. I cleared my throat. I slammed my book shut. But I always froze when they turned toward me.

Cool! I thought. *This is fun.*

Miranda walked into the dining room with Fern and Jasmine. That was my cue to open the book and turn the pages slowly. And that was Campbell's cue to scream.

My heart raced as I flipped open the book.

"It's alive!" Campbell shrieked as I turned the pages. "The portrait of Prudence Whitehead is alive!"

Peering over my glasses, I could see Miranda. She had a funny look on her face as she stared at me.

It's working, I thought excitedly. *They're totally horrified!*

But then I felt my nose begin to tickle. *Oh, no!* I thought. *I can't sneeze. Not now!*

I sniffed and wiggled my nose. But it was no use. My head whipped back, and I let out a giant, *Ah-ah-ah-chooooooo!*

My head jerked forward. And the gray wig dropped right into my lap!

"Hey, look!" a girl called out. "Isn't that Mary-Kate Burke from the First Form?"

"It has to be!" another said. "She is *so* funny!"

The next thing I knew, tons of kids were pointing and laughing. But Miranda was not amused. She frowned and muttered something to her friends.

Uh-oh, I thought. *Strike two!*

Dear Diary,

Today Phoebe, Campbell, and I turned the Warwick House kitchen into Dr. D. Kay's Mad Laboratory.

There were rows of beakers filled with green slime and bubbles floating everywhere. It's amazing what you can do with instant pistachio pudding and green balloons.

"This room is awesome!" I declared.

Phoebe nodded as she ironed a white lab coat smeared with red paint that looked just like blood. "The committee will definitely approve."

"Woo-hoo!" Campbell cheered. She waved the mad-scientist wig in the air. "Hair-Raiser House, here we come!"

Mary-Kate was in the room helping us blow up balloons. And everyone knew her big acting job was on the line.

"Whoops. Sorry, Mary-Kate," Campbell murmured.

"Don't worry. You can still think of something!" I told my sister.

The balloon squeaked as Mary-Kate tied a knot in it.

"It's Wednesday night." She sighed. "The Hair-Raiser Committee probably made up their minds already. I don't have a chance."

The door opened, and Dana walked into the kitchen. "News flash, everyone," she announced. "Miranda wants all of us to report to the old history building right now."

"That place hasn't been used in years," I said.

"Why does she want us to go there?" Campbell asked.

Dana narrowed her eyes. "Why do you *think* she wants us to go there?" she asked. "Hmmmm?"

The bowl of instant green pudding shook a little in my hands. I'd been having so much fun that I'd forgotten all about Fright Night!

"Ashley?" Dana tilted her head as she studied me. "Are you okay?"

"Me?" I squealed. "I'm—"

POP!

A balloon burst, and I jumped!

"Come on," Mary-Kate told us. "Let's just go and get this over with."

It was eight o'clock as the five of us left Dr. D. Kay's Mad Laboratory. Leaves crunched and twigs snapped as we trudged across the dark campus. We were the only ones outside. It seemed to get even darker as we neared the old history building.

"We are *so* doomed!" Dana said. "If I never get out alive, I want all my clothes to go to Kristen. And my makeup to Brooke. And my shoes—"

"Dana, will you shut up already?" Campbell snapped.

My heart pounded as we walked up the path to the big brick building. There were no lights inside. No sounds, either.

Mary-Kate stepped up to the wooden door with the cracked, peeling paint. She reached out and knocked. Once. Twice. Three times.

We waited a few seconds.

A deep moan came from an upstairs window.

"Oh, what a shame. Nobody's home!" I said quickly. "Now we'll have to go all the way back—"

Suddenly the door swung open—all by itself!

The front hall was dark. We all stared at one another, unsure of what to do next. Everything was silent. Creepy quiet.

Then someone screamed.

Chapter 6

Thursday

Dear Diary,

My knees were shaking like jelly. *Should I go in? Or run for my life?* I wondered.

Miranda appeared from the darkness. She was wearing all black. She silently waved us all inside.

"You can still get out of this, Ashley," Dana whispered in my ear. "All you have to do is turn around."

Diary, I was never so torn in my life.

"Ashley, we got this far," Mary-Kate said. "Let's just go for it!"

"O-okay," I said. But I still wasn't sure.

Mary-Kate placed her hand on the doorknob. A few cobwebs fluttered down as she slowly opened the door. She led the way as we filed inside.

"I can't see a thing," Phoebe whispered. "It's so dark in here."

Bats! I thought. *Bats hang out in the dark!*

"It's cold, too!" Campbell said.

Ghosts! I thought. *Haunted houses are always cold. Or at least they are in the movies.*

"Do you get the feeling that we're not alone?" Mary-Kate asked.

I heard a rustle. Then the lights flashed on and— "SURPRISE!"

I blinked from the bright lights. Miranda and the other Warwick girls were in the room. They were wearing feathery tiaras and goofy party hats!

I looked around for bats or ghosts. Instead, I saw more girls from different forms. And balloons, paper streamers, and a table loaded with chips, dip, and pink punch! "It's a party!" I gasped.

Diary, I was never so relieved in my whole life. But why would the Hair-Raiser Committee throw a party for us wanna-bes?

"Congratulations!" Miranda announced. "You've passed your tests. You get to work on Hair-Raiser House!"

Everyone cheered.

"Wait a minute!" I called to the Warwick girls. "You mean you guys aren't going to scare us?"

The girls looked at one another. "Where did you get that idea?" Miranda asked.

I turned and glared at Dana. She gave me a little smirk.

"Dana lied," I said to Mary-Kate through gritted teeth. But my sister seemed too happy to care about Dana.

"Ashley, I'm in!" she cried. "I'm really in!"

That's when it hit me, too. The Warwick girls liked my scripts. And Mary-Kate had passed her initiation, too!

"You're all in!" Miranda said again. "*Except* Mary-Kate!"

"Except me?" Mary-Kate squeaked.

"We really don't want to dump you, Mary-Kate," Miranda explained. "So you have one more chance to try to scare us."

I could feel my sister's pain. And embarrassment. Her face was bright red. "Gee, thanks," Mary-Kate said, forcing a smile.

"Okay, everybody!" Miranda shouted. She raised a fist in the air. "What are we waiting for? Let's get this party started!"

A 4-You song began to pulse through the room. Some girls danced. Others headed for the snack table. But Phoebe, Campbell, and I gathered around Mary-Kate.

"Hey, it's not so bad, Mary-Kate," Phoebe said. "You still have a chance to work on Hair-Raiser House."

"I know," Mary-Kate said. "It's cool."

But what Dana had done wasn't *cool!* I thought.

"Okay, Woletsky, what's the deal?" I demanded as she walked by. "Why did you tell us the Warwick girls were going to scare us?"

Dana shrugged. "I was hoping you'd wimp out, Ashley," she said. "So Kristen could take your place."

"Why me?" I cried.

"In the assembly I heard Mary-Kate call you a chicken," Dana said. "So I figured if anyone would drop out, it'd be you. But you wouldn't have if you had known about the party."

"You knew about the party all along?" Campbell asked.

"Yep," Dana said. "That's what I really heard when I brought back Miranda's laundry."

"That was low, Dana!" I snapped. "How could you do such a thing?"

"I did it to get Kristen in," Dana said. "That's what best friends are for, right?"

My cheeks began to burn.

"Besides," Dana went on, "watching you freak out every time I mentioned Fright Night made it even more worthwhile!"

Now my face burned all the way down to my neck. Not only had Dana lied—she'd made a total jerk out of me!

"How would you like it if someone did that to you, Dana?" Mary-Kate asked.

"It would never happen," Dana said. "Because nothing scares me. I've got nerves of steel!"

"Oh, yeah?" I said. "Well, I'm going to find a way to scare you. Even if it's the last thing I do!"

Dana tossed her hair over her shoulder and laughed. "I'd like to see you try!" She gave us a little princess wave and walked away.

"Do you really think you can scare her, Ashley?" Phoebe asked.

I pictured Dana screaming with terror. It would be the *perfect* revenge. "Just wait and see," I said. "In no time I'll have Dana 'Nerves of Steel' Woletsky shaking in her designer boots!"

Dear Diary,

Today I felt like I was on a wild roller-coaster ride. First I thought I was *out* of Hair-Raiser House. Then I was back *in*. And now I'm not actually in yet—but it's still possible!

"I only have one more chance, Elise," I said as we walked to our English class this morning. "So I have to come up with something good!"

"What do you have so far?" Elise asked.

"Well," I said, "I can deliver a gorgeous flower

arrangement to Miranda—with a swarm of bees inside!"

"You would never do that," Elise said, shaking her head. "Too dangerous."

"I know." I sighed. "Besides, where would I find all those bees at the end of October?"

"What else?" Elise asked.

"I could write 'Beware Miranda' on her mirror with lipstick!" I said. "Do you think that would freak her out?"

"Only if it's her own lip-stick," Elise said. "She pays a fortune for that stuff."

I groaned. What good was having another chance when all my ideas tanked?

"It'll be bad enough if I don't get into Hair-Raiser House," I said. "But if I blow it again, the whole school will think I can't act!"

"You *can* act, Mary-Kate," Elise assured me. "And you will think of something!"

Elise stopped in front of a flier tacked to a bulletin board. "Cool! The Friday night movie this week is Volleyball Vampire Part Two!" she exclaimed.

I studied the flyer. It showed a picture of girls playing volleyball—and all the girls had fangs!

"A vampire named Count Spectacula turns an entire high school volleyball team into vampires!"

Elise said. "It's a movie classic!"

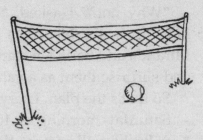

"Volleyball, huh?" I asked. I looked at the flyer again. "Miranda and her friends are on the volleyball team."

Elise giggled. "Really? Then they'd better watch out for Count Spectacula!"

That gave me an idea. I turned and stared at Elise.

"What?" Elise asked. "Do I have lip gloss on my teeth or something?"

I shook my head. "Elise, how would I look in fangs?" I asked.

"Excuse me?" Elise said.

I glanced over my shoulder. All over campus, kids were hurrying to their classes.

"Miranda's volleyball team practices every Saturday morning," I told Elise. "So this Saturday morning I'll give them a little scare!"

"How are you going to do that?" Elise asked.

"I'll get some creepy vampire makeup from the drama department," I explained. "And a black cape, a pair of fake fangs—

"Mary-Kate!" Elise laughed. "You're not thinking of becoming Count Spectacula—are you?"

"Why not?" I asked. "He's totally spooky! I'll hide up in the bleachers in the gym. As soon as Miranda and her team start practicing, I'll jump out and surprise them as a vampire!"

So that's the plan, Diary.

Saturday morning at 10:00 A.M. sharp, I, Mary-Kate Burke, will become Volleyball Vampire . . . Part Three!

And this time I *won't* mess up!

Chapter 7

Friday

Dear Diary,

Thinking up ways to scare Dana isn't that hard. I'm getting lots of practice writing those spooky scripts for Hair-Raiser House.

"What have you got so far, Ashley?" Phoebe asked this morning as we walked through the science building. She was on her way to chemistry class. I was biology-bound.

"Remember those rubber rats we're putting in the Hair-Raiser Dungeon Room?" I asked.

"Rats?" Phoebe gasped. "You're not going to use a real rat to scare Dana, are you?"

A shiver ran up my back. If there is anything I hated more than worms and bugs, it's rats! "No way!" I said. "But I do know where I can find a little white mouse."

Phoebe raised an eyebrow. "You mean like the ones in your biology classroom?"

"Right!" I said. I stopped in front of the biology lab. "And mice just love to crawl where they don't belong. Like inside Dana's backpack!"

I waved good-bye to Phoebe and walked into the

bio lab. Most of the kids were gazing into micro-scopes. Dana was staring into a pocket mirror and putting on mascara.

"Today we're looking at protozoan," Mr. Barber, our biology teacher, was saying. "As you know, those are microscopic, single-cell animals."

I walked toward my seat, but as soon as Mr. Barber started writing on the board, I headed straight to Victor Nichols—the class science whiz. Victor is so smart, he gets to work on his own exper-iments. And this week his experiment included *mice*!

"Hi, Victor," I said.

Victor glanced up from the clipboard he was

holding. On one side of his counter was a mini TV. On the other was a cage. I tried not to look at the two mice running around inside.

"Oh!" Victor said in a surprised voice. "Hi, Ashley!"

"How's your mice experiment coming along?" I asked.

"Super!" Victor exclaimed. "As you can see, the mouse placed in front of the TV ate more cheese than the mouse who was not in front of the TV."

"Really?" I tried to sound interested.

"Which proves that snack-food commercials

have a profound effect on one's appetite!" Victor replied.

One of the mice squeaked, and I jumped.

"Here!" Victor said. He stuck his hand in the cage. "Feel how fat this little guy got!"

"No, thanks!" I blurted out. "I don't touch . . . mice."

"Oh," Victor said, disappointed.

"But I do need your help, Victor," I whispered. "I want to scare Dana Woletsky."

Victor glanced at Dana across the room. "She stuck a wad of chewed-up gum on my microscope slide once," he said. "It spoiled my whole experiment in mold reproduction."

I nodded. "Then you know why scaring Dana is so important."

"What do you want me to do?" Victor whispered.

"Simple," I whispered back. "Stick one of your mice into Dana's backpack."

"Just one mouse?" Victor asked. He rubbed his hands together. "How about a whole handful of fly larvae?"

That gross thought made me gag. "Um, one mouse is plenty, thanks," I said.

Victor reached into the cage and pulled out the fat mouse. "We'll use Willard," he said. He held it out to me.

"Yuck." I turned my head away. "You just hurry up and do it."

Victor cupped Willard in both hands. Then he tiptoed over to Dana's backpack. It was lying next to her feet. In a flash he slipped the wiggling white mouse under the flap.

"Mission accomplished!" Victor said when he came back. "Who's going to tell her—you or me?"

"Oh, I'll do the honors, Victor," I said sweetly.

I smiled as I walked over to Dana, who was still checking herself out in the mirror. I couldn't wait to watch her freak!

"Hi, Dana," I said. "Are you discovering a cure for split ends? Or the common zit?"

"Cute," Dana said. She put down her mirror and looked into the microscope on the lab table.

"I hate to tell you this," I went on. "But I think something white and furry just crawled into your backpack."

This time Dana looked at me. "I don't believe you," she said.

"Fine." I shrugged. "Look in your backpack and see for yourself."

Dana rolled her eyes. She stood and reached down for her backpack. She lifted it up onto the high counter and stuck her hand deep inside the bag.

Perfect! I thought. *In a few seconds Dana will be screaming her head off!*

But as Dana pulled Willard out of her backpack, she began to smile and coo. "Oh! What a sweet little thing. Just like Stuart Little!" She started petting the mouse.

"What?" I cried. Dana wasn't scared of the mouse—she *loved* it!

"Here, Ashley," Dana said. She held the mouse out to me. "He wants to say hi!"

Before I could protest Dana shoved Willard into my hands. "Eeeeek!" I screamed. "Get it off me!"

"What is going on here?" Mr. Barber demanded.

I dropped Willard onto the counter, and he ran around in circles. The whole class laughed as Victor tried to snatch him up.

"Nice try, Ashley," Dana said. "But, like I said, nerves of steel. Remember?"

How could this happen, Diary? I didn't scare Dana. I just scared *myself!*

Dear Diary,

Guess what? I actually got my hands on a long, flowing black cape!

"Ta-daaa!" I sang as I twirled around.

Elise sat on my bed as I modeled my Count

Spectacula costume. My face was painted white, my lips were bright red, and my hair was slicked back with shiny black gel.

"That cape is awesome!" Elise said. "You're lucky the drama department had one!"

"I didn't get it in the drama department," I said.

"Then where?" Elise asked.

"Phoebe Cahill's closet," I answered. "It's amazing what you can find in there!"

I popped a pair of white plastic fangs in my mouth.

"This is just a dress rehearsal for tomorrow," I said through the fangs, "but what do you think?"

"Not very glamorous," Elise said. "But scary!"

Scary! The word that I wanted to hear!

"Vonderful!" I said in my best vampire voice. "I vont to scare the Vhite Oak volleyball team!"

Chapter 8

Saturday

Dear Diary,

I've learned two things since that biology class disaster yesterday.

One: The only mouse I'm ever going to touch again is the one attached to my computer.

Two: Scaring Dana "Nerves of Steel" Woletsky isn't going to be as easy as I'd thought!

But right now I have to write more scary scripts for Hair-Raiser House.

"Read the next one, Ashley," Phoebe said.

"Yeah!" Campbell said. "So far, you're doing great."

My friends were hanging up fake cobwebs around Queen Vampira's Cave. I was sitting on the vampire's cardboard coffin with my Hair-Raiser notebook on my lap.

"The next scene takes place in a dark, dusty room filled with old furniture, stuffed birds, and drippy candles," I said. "Everyone sits behind a round table and holds hands. Madame Ashlinka contacts the spirits."

"You mean, like a séance?" Phoebe asked.

I smiled and nodded.

"That'll be so cool!" Campbell exclaimed. She wrapped a lamp with more cobwebs. "We can get someone to stand outside the window. And make creepy noises at the right parts!"

"Perfect," Phoebe said. "A séance will scare anybody."

I looked up from my notebook. "Anybody?" I asked. "As in . . . Dana? Do you think a séance would scare her?"

"Ashley, we like the *idea* of a séance," Phoebe said, "but nobody *believes* in them."

"And Dana won't, either," Campbell agreed.

"She will if we do it right!" I jumped up off the coffin. "First we'll turn off the lights and rig the room with creepy sound effects. Then we'll all act scared as if we really did contact a spirit!"

Phoebe and Campbell looked at each other. Then they smiled.

"It does sound like fun," Phoebe admitted. "We can round up a bunch of our friends to help."

"And I'll hide outside and do the creepy sound effects!" Campbell added.

"Great!" I said. "Let's have the séance in the Porter House lounge tomorrow night, while everyone else is at the ice-cream sundae party in the dining room."

"We're going to miss the ice-cream sundae party?" Campbell complained. "Hey, I wanted to go to that."

"This will be more fun," I promised. "And less fattening."

Diary, I can't wait! We already have the big round table, the extra friends, and the drippy candles.

Now all we need is Dana Woletsky!

Dear Diary,

There I was, Saturday morning at 9:55, dressed up as Count Spectacula and crouched under the top steps of the bleachers. The air in the gym was warm and damp. I could feel my black hair gel and white makeup start to drip.

Any minute now, I thought as I clutched the cape around my shoulders. *Any minute Miranda and her team are going to walk into the gym.*

I heard voices outside the heavy steel door. Then the door opened.

"Let's do some serves before Coach Katz gets here," a voice said. It sounded like Miranda.

I peeked between the steps. I saw Miranda and her team taking positions on both sides of the net.

Miranda held the volleyball in one hand while she raised her other arm to serve. I ducked back under the bleachers. I couldn't let her see me yet!

The ball thumped as Miranda punched it hard.

Okay, I thought. *It's now or never.*

Taking a deep breath, I jumped up on the bleachers.

"Ahhhh-voooo!" I howled, waving my arms in the air. "Ahhhh-voooo!"

A few girls shrieked as I flapped my cape and raced down the steps.

It's working! I thought. *They really think I'm Count Spectacula!*

But just as I reached the bottom, the heel of my shoe got caught on the hem of my cape. I went flying across the gym!

"Ahhh!" I shouted. I prepared for a crash landing. Luckily I fell with thud on a padded tumbling mat.

When I finally opened my eyes, I saw the volleyball team standing around me and staring.

"It's Mary-Kate Burke again!" a girl said.

"Mary-Kate!" Miranda said. "When are you going to give up this clown act?"

I opened my mouth to answer. But I was too humiliated to speak!

"Sorry." Miranda shook her head. "It's pretty obvious that you're *not* going to prove yourself."

The girls on the team walked back to the net, laughing. All I could do was stare up at the ceiling.

That was my last chance.

And I had blown it!

Chapter 9

Sunday

Dear Diary,

The hard part wasn't getting Dana to come to the séance—it was getting her to *stay*!

"What am I doing here?" Dana complained. "I could be at that ice-cream sundae party right now."

I looked around at Phoebe, Elise, and Summer. We were all about to scare the living daylights out of Dana. And we couldn't wait!

"I told you a million times, Dana," I said. "If we're going to hold a fake séance at Hair-Raiser House, we have to rehearse our lines."

I passed copies of the script around the table.

"Now remember," I said. "Holding hands in a circle is part of the séance. That way, we can pretend to pass energy to one another—and to the spirits!"

"Yes, Madame Ashlinka!" Summer giggled.

The room was dark except for one flickering candle on the table. It gave my friends' faces an eerie glow.

"If everyone has a copy of the script," I said, "let's get started."

We joined hands.

"Concentrate on the spirit world," I said. "And I, Madame Ashlinka, will guide you."

"Give me a break," Dana muttered.

I closed my eyes and swayed back and forth. "'I sense the presence of a spirit now!'" I declared. "'Can everyone feel the energy?'"

"'I feel a spirit is entering my mind right now!'" Summer read from her script. "'Rock back and forth.'"

"'Rock back and forth' are the stage directions, Summer!" Wendy groaned.

"Oops," Summer said. "Sorry."

"'I am the channel for a spirit named Annabelle,'" Phoebe read. "'She is very lonely. She wants us to be her friends.'"

"Spare me!" Dana snorted. "No one believes in these stupid things."

You *will soon*, I thought.

"'Spirits!'" I cried. "'If you are with us in this room, give us a sign *now*!'"

Everyone waited in silence. Until—

RAP! RAP! RAP!

"What was that?" Dana asked, frowning. "The script doesn't say anything about weird noises."

I smiled to myself. Campbell was doing a great job tapping on the window.

"It's the spirits!" I cried. "They have sent us a sign that they are among us!"

"Ooooh!" Wendy exclaimed. "I am very, very scared."

"So am I!" Elise said. She put a hand to her forehead. "If the spirits are evil, then what is to become of us?"

I cringed. Elise was really laying it on thick. Then I peeked at Dana. She had a very serious look on her face.

RAP! RAP! RAP!

"There it is again!" Dana cried.

Good job, Campbell, I thought. But then the door opened a crack— and Campbell peeked inside!

What's Campbell doing in here, I wondered, *when she should be out there?*

Campbell frowned and shook her head. She had something to tell me!

"C-close your eyes—quick!" I told the others. "And concentrate on the spirit world!"

"Hey!" Summer said. "That's not in the script."

"Just close your eyes!" I snapped.

When everyone's eyes were shut, Campbell hurried over to me. "Mrs. Viola made me come inside," she whispered in my ear. "I never got to rap on the window. Or do anything!"

I stared at Campbell.

"You weren't making those creepy noises?" I whispered. "So who was?"

RAP! RAP! RAP!

"Eeeee!" I shrieked.

The others opened their eyes and stared at me.

"The séance worked!" I cried. "There are spirits in the room with us!"

Summer pointed at Campbell. "What's she doing in here? I thought she was supposed to be outside making creepy—"

Phoebe clapped her hand over Summer's mouth. "Oh, those spirits!" She chuckled. "The things they make us say!"

But it didn't matter anymore. We were being haunted now—for real!

"Campbell wasn't doing anything!" I said. "So the noises must be coming from spirits. *Real* spirits!"

RAP! RAP! RAP!

Everyone gasped. But Dana eyed me suspiciously. "Spirits, huh?" Dana got up and walked to the window. She pulled back the curtain and laughed.

"There's your stupid spirit, Ashley. A tree branch!"

"A . . . what?" I asked.

I joined Dana by the window and peered outside. A heavy tree branch was swinging back and forth in the wind. And it was rapping against the window!

"Maybe the spirits . . . are swinging on the tree branches?" I said with a weak smile.

Dana smirked. "I told you, Ashley. You can't scare me."

I watched in horror as Dana left the room, laughing.

I just don't get it, Diary!

I can write great articles for the school paper and spooky scenes for Hair-Raiser House. I can bake the best cookies at White Oak. I can even do a perfect pirouette in ballet class.

Why can't I scare Dana Woletsky?

Dear Diary,

I refuse to give up! I *can* be scary. I *can* pass this audition. I *can* scare the com- mittee!

"I know," I told myself as I paced my room. "I'll plant a rubber snake inside Miranda's gym sneaker. No—I can pretend my glow-in-the-dark Frisbee is a UFO! I can sneak into Miranda's room and—"

There was a knock at the door and Cheryl came in. "What on earth are you trying to be now?" she asked.

I spun around to show off my latest costume. I was wearing a pair of pointy ears, a long tail, and wings. And I was covered with gray powder. "I'm one of the gargoyles from the dining hall!" I said through my plastic fangs.

Everyone at White Oak knows about the gargoyles in the dining hall. They're those ugly, winged creatures that stare down at us from the ceiling.

"All I have to do is hide in the dining hall," I explained. "Then when everyone comes in for the ice-cream sundae party, I'll spread my wings and—"

KNOCK, KNOCK, KNOCK.

"Who is it?" Cheryl called as she headed for the door.

"Cheryl—don't open it!" I said. "I don't want anyone to see my costume yet!"

Too late. Cheryl had already opened the door. And Stacey from the Hair-Raiser Committee was standing outside.

"Mary-Kate?" Stacey said, staring at me. "Miranda wants you in the Warwick House lounge right away." She looked me up and down, then giggled.

"I'll be there," I promised.

Stacey left, still giggling.

"I wonder what that's all about?" Cheryl asked.

My stomach did a triple flip. I was pretty sure I knew the answer!

Chapter 10

Sunday

Dear Diary,

So there I was. Sitting before the Hair-Raiser Committee in a gargoyle costume.

Miranda stood. "I'm sorry, Mary-Kate," she said. "But we've decided that you're not Hair-Raiser House material."

The other girls nodded in agreement. They must have thought I was a big joke, too.

My heart sank. First I don't get a part in the play. And now this!

"But we did find a replacement for you," Miranda said. As if I cared. "She's from the First Form. Her name is Valerie Metcalf."

I mouth dropped open, and my fangs fell out. "Valerie?" I gasped. "But she's playing the lead in *Our Town!*"

"I know," Miranda said with a smile. "Valerie wanted to work on Hair-Raiser House so bad that she's making time for both!"

This was too much for me to take!

"Valerie's a super actress," Miranda went on. "We're so psyched about working with her."

Dare to Scare

The wings on my costume drooped. I had just been totally humiliated. And I was about to become Hair-Raiser history. But for now I was going to stay cool. "I'm sorry things didn't work out." I walked toward the door. "But I understand. Really."

"Good!" Miranda said. "By the way, Mary-Kate. What were you trying to be this time? Some kind of . . . flying squirrel?"

Miranda and her friends didn't even know a gargoyle when they saw one. But I just smiled a little and said, "Something like that."

"Cute!" Miranda said.

As I dragged my tail all the way back to Porter House, I knew my worst fear had come true. I'd failed the audition—and had been booted from Hair-Raiser House.

But all isn't lost, Diary.

I can still pitch a perfect softball. Let's see Valerie Metcalf do *that*!

Dear Diary,

I couldn't stop thinking about Dana all morning. Not even when I was sitting next to my boyfriend, Ross, in art history class.

"The Egyptian pyramids were built as magnificent tombs," our teacher, Ms. Kellogg, was saying.

"They housed mummies and worldly possessions."

I barely heard Ms. Kellogg as she flashed one slide after another on the screen.

Maybe nothing does *scare Dana*, I thought. *Maybe she really does have nerves of steel.*

Ross nudged my arm. "Check that out," he whispered.

"What?" I whispered back.

"The mummy," Ross said.

I looked at the screen. The slide showed a stiff figure wrapped in some decaying material. "Gross." I giggled. "It looks like a week-old burrito left out in the sun."

"Yeah." Ross snickered. "How'd you like to find one of those in your closet?"

I remembered a movie I once saw. It was about a mummy who escaped his tomb to terrorize a whole kingdom. Mary-Kate had liked it. But I had been so scared, I couldn't sleep for a week!

Wait a minute! I thought. *What would Dana do if she found a mummy inside her closet?*

"Thanks, Ross!" I said.

"For what?" Ross asked, surprised.

"For giving me the most awesome and brilliant idea!" I replied.

Diary, it was worth a shot! So during midday

break, Phoebe, Campbell, and I went straight to Dana's room with bags of bandages. But before we could scare Dana, we had to deal with Dana's roommate—Lisa Dunmead.

"So when will Dana be back, Lisa?" I asked.

Lisa stood at the door and said, "Dana went to get her mail. She'll be back in about fifteen minutes."

Fifteen minutes! That gave me practically no time to wrap myself up and hide in Dana's closet!

"Why do you want to know?" Lisa asked.

"Oh, we want to play a little joke on Dana," I said. "I'm going to fall out of her closet wrapped like a mummy."

Lisa blinked. "That's a joke?"

"An *inside* joke!" Phoebe said. "We've been telling mummy jokes at Hair-Raiser House all week!"

"Yeah!" Campbell said. "Like, 'What's a mummy's favorite sandwich?'"

Lisa shrugged.

"A wrap!" Campbell said. "Get it?"

"So what do you say?" I asked Lisa.

"Sounds kind of lame to me," Lisa said. She started to shut the door.

"Wait, Lisa!" I slammed my hand against the door. "We need your help."

"My help?" Lisa asked.

"We need you here when Dana gets back," I explained. "So you can get her to open the closet!"

"I don't think—" Lisa began.

"And we need you to help us wrap up Ashley like a mummy!" Campbell interrupted.

Lisa looked at me. Then she smiled slowly. "Now that sounds like fun!" she said.

I shot Campbell a glare as we entered the room.

"Hey, I got us in, didn't I?" Campbell whispered.

Phoebe dumped the rolls of bandages on the pink shaggy rug in the center of the room. "It's a good thing the school nurse was generous," she told me, "or we'd be wrapping you with toilet paper."

I didn't like the idea of being wrapped from head to toe with anything. But I *did* like the idea of scaring Dana!

"Hold still," Campbell said.

I was dressed in a black leo-tard and matching tights. As I stood between the two beds, the others started winding the ban-dages. Campbell worked on one leg, Phoebe the other. Lisa wrapped me from my waist up.

"Do I really get to wrap your face?" Lisa asked.

"Okay—but leave enough space for my mouth!"

I warned Lisa. "And my nose! And my eyes!"

After a few more minutes they were finally done.

"That's a wrap!" Campbell joked. She shrugged. "Another mummy joke."

It wasn't easy smiling underneath all those bandages. Or talking! "How do I look?" I mumbled.

"Go to the mirror and see for yourself," Phoebe said.

Easy for her to say! The bandages were so tight, I had to hop my way to the full-length mirror. But when I finally got there, I liked what I saw. "Cool!" I said. "I look totally mummy-ish!"

"Dana will be back any minute, Ashley," Lisa said. "So you'd better get into her closet fast!"

Lisa helped me hop to Dana's closet. But when she opened it, I gasped. It was stuffed with tons of clothes and accessories!

"Look at all this stuff!" I cried. "There's no room for me!"

"Yes, there is," Lisa said. I felt her hand on my back as she shoved me inside the closet. Now I was stuffed between hanging pants, skirts, dresses, and jackets!

"I'll leave it open just a crack," Phoebe said, shutting the door.

"Good luck, Ashley," Campbell told me.

Phoebe shut the closet door almost all the way. The shoe bag hanging on the inside was inches away from my face!

From inside the closet I heard Campbell and Phoebe scurry toward the door.

"Remember, Lisa," Phoebe was saying. "Get Dana to open her closet."

"And don't forget to scream!" Campbell added.

"I got it, I got it," Lisa said.

I heard the door to the hall open, then close.

"Hey, Ashley?" Lisa called through the closet door. "How are you doing in there?"

"G-g-great!" I stammered.

But I really wasn't. I hate cramped spaces—especially *dark* cramped spaces.

The bandages began to itch—like a million ants marching up and down my legs and arms. And the smell of Dana's sneakers was enough to make me gag! "Lisa—get me out of here!" I whispered.

"Oh, hi, Dana!" I heard Lisa say. "Anything good in the mail?"

I held my breath. Dana was in the room!

"Yeah, check out this new catalog," Dana said. "The clothes are so cool!"

"Um," Lisa said, "speaking of clothes—can I borrow your denim jacket? The one with the brown fur collar?"

"Sure," Dana said. "It's in the closet."

"*Where* in the closet?" Lisa asked.

Hmm, I thought. *Good job, Lisa!*

"Lisa!" Dana sighed. "It's right here!"

The closet door swung open.

Dana jumped back as my stiff body fell forward. First I hit the shaggy pink rug. Then an avalanche of sweaters, shoe boxes, and handbags landed on me!

"Ow!" A wooden sandal bounced off my arm. But I couldn't waste time. I had to terrorize Dana!

I wiggled and managed to flip over. "Daaaana!" I moaned in a creepy voice. "You dare to open my tomb. I cast a curse upon thee!"

I tried to stand up but couldn't. I was too tightly wrapped!

"Daaaaana!" I tried again.

"Oh, spare me!" Dana groaned. "It's Ashley trying to be scary again."

Come on, Lisa, I said silently. *Scream—or something!*

"I told her it sounded lame," Lisa said.

"Ashley, Ashley, Ashley." Dana sighed. "Why don't you just give it up already?"

I glared at Dana between my bandages. But deep inside I wondered if she was right. Maybe I *should* give up!

"Hey, look!" Lisa suddenly exclaimed. She

kneeled down and pointed next to my shoulder. "It's the denim jacket I wanted to borrow!"

Lisa grabbed the jacket. Then she and Dana bopped out of the room together.

I wiggled my hips as I tried to stand up. But all I could do was flip over on my stomach.

I was stuck!

"Somebody!" I yelled. "Heeeelp!"

Chapter 11

Tuesday

Dear Diary,

It's been two days since I got the boot from Hair-Raiser House, and I'm still bummed out. But when I met up with Ashley in the TV room after dinner tonight, she wasn't doing much better!

"What's wrong with me, Mary-Kate?" Ashley said. "I can't believe I still haven't scared Dana!"

More kids came into the TV room. Some sat on folding chairs. Others plopped into stuffed beanbags. Ashley and I were sharing the small brown sofa against the wall.

"And I can't believe I'm out of Hair-Raiser House." I gave a big sigh. "Let's face it, Ashley. Maybe we're just not scary, that's all."

My eyes darted around the room. I saw two colorful posters pinned to the bulletin board. One was for Hair-Raiser House. The other was for *Our Town* starring Valerie Metcalf. Two reminders that I was a major loser!

I looked away from the posters and stared blankly at the TV. It was turned to *Name That Jingle*—a show where people win prizes by naming commercial tunes.

It isn't my favorite show—or Ashley's. But we

needed something goofy to take our minds off our problems.

"Mary-Kate," Ashley muttered. "Look who's here!"

I turned to see Dana and Kristen strutting into the room.

"Just ignore them," I whispered.

"Welcome to *Name That Jingle!*" David Barnett, the show's host, announced. "Meet our two new contestants: Jim, from New York City, and Marion, from Grand Rapids, Michigan."

Dana and Kristen sat down in canvas butterfly chairs.

"You might recognize this first tune," the host went on. "But who was the *sweet* little guy who sang it?"

"Remote, please!" Dana groaned. "This show is *sooo* stupid. Let's watch *Starstruck!*"

I glanced at Ashley. Then I carefully slipped the remote under the sofa cushion.

"What part of 'boring' don't you understand, people?" Dana asked everyone. "Wouldn't you rather watch—"

"Delightful Doughnuts are so sweet!" a perky voice sang out. "Just the thing when you need a treat."

Dana's body stiffened as she stared at the TV.

"Marion for ten points," the host announced. "What favorite character sings that tune?"

"Is it Dougie the Delightful Doughnut Boy?" Marion cried.

"Dougie is correct!" David declared. "Congratulations, Marion. Now let's give it up for the Delightful Doughnut Boy!"

The TV audience cheered as a guy dressed in a white baker's hat and smock ran onto the stage. He had a powdered-sugar face, doughnut eyes, and a cherry nose. "Delightful Doughnuts are so sweet!" he sang. "Just the thing when you need a—"

"Iced tea!" Dana cried as she jumped up. "I need a can of iced tea—now!"

She hurried past the beverage machine—and out the door!

"That was weird," Ashley said.

"Yeah," I agreed. "What made Dana bolt like that?"

Kristen overheard us talking. "Dana's been scared of that Delightful Doughnut Boy ever since she was five," she explained. "Dana flips every time she sees him." She turned back to the TV.

"Did you hear that?" I whispered.

"I sure did," Ashley replied. "And now I finally know how to scare Miss Nerves of Steel!"

Dear Diary,

By 9:30 tonight, most of the girls at White Oak were in their dorms, waiting for lights-out. But Phoebe and I were outside, leading the Hair-Raiser Committee into a woodsy part of campus.

It was all part of the plot to scare Dana. And Mary-Kate was going to help!

"It's freezing out here!" Dana complained. "What are we doing in the woods anyway?"

"Dana's right," Miranda told us. "What's the deal already?"

I smiled at Phoebe as she lit the way with a flashlight. The Fifth Formers had been asking me that question since we'd left Warwick House.

"We came up with something really cool for Hair-Raiser House," I told them. "After the visitors leave the house, we'll take them on a haunted hayride through the woods."

"A hayride? You mean those things they have for little kids at petting zoos?" Stacey asked.

"No, no, no!" Phoebe said. "This hayride would run into all kinds of spooky stuff in the woods."

"And at the end we can serve hot apple cider or

cocoa," I suggested. "And maybe cookies and sandwiches. Everyone can sit on bales of hay."

"No can do, Ashley," Miranda told me. "Halloween is less than three days away. We don't have enough time to set everything up."

I pretended to look disappointed.

"And what spooky stuff would we see on a hayride, anyway?" Dana asked. "Scarecrows?"

"It was just a suggestion," I said.

"Yeah—a bad one." Dana turned to the committee. "Let's go."

"Fine with me," Miranda said.

As they began to leave, I gave Phoebe a nod. She nodded back, then flicked off her flashlight.

"Hey! What happened to the light?" Dana complained.

"It's pitch-black!" Jasmine cried.

"Not funny, Phoebe," Miranda said. "Turn that thing back on and let's get out of here."

"Can't," Phoebe said. "The battery must have died."

Dana groaned. "What's the matter, Phoebe? Is your flashlight vintage, too?"

"Okay, okay," Miranda said, trying to stay calm. "Is anyone else carrying a flashlight? A penlight? Glow-in-the-dark lipstick?"

Nobody answered.

"Just great!" Fern complained. "Now how are we going to get out of—"

SNAP! SNAP! SNAP!

"What was that?" Miranda asked nervously.

I smiled to myself. Mary-Kate was right on time!

"Oh, no!" I wailed. "Something's coming!"

Chapter 12

Wednesday

Dear Diary,

It was dark, so no one could see me. But I hid just in case. A bunch of twigs broke as I ran behind another tree.

SNAP! SNAP! SNAP!

"There it is again!" Stacey gasped.

"This is just like those Jarad movies!" Miranda moaned. "He's always sneaking up on people in the woods!"

"Quit it, Miranda!" Jasmine said. "Let's just go home!"

I listened for Dana's voice. Was she scared yet?

"Hel-lo?" Dana chuckled in the dark. "This is the woods. It's probably some poor little animal!"

 I peeked out from behind the tree. A glow-in-the-dark skeleton suddenly dropped down from a nearby tree. Its arms and legs flopped as it bobbed up and down in the air.

The committee shrieked.

"Help!" Miranda cried.

But Dana still didn't seem scared. "Glow-in-the-dark is cool," she said.

"At least the skeleton gives us some light now, right?"

That does it, I thought. "Ooooh!" I began to moan.

"Now what?" Miranda asked.

"Oooh!" I moaned again, louder.

"Run!" Stacey cried.

I turned on the old-fashioned lantern I was holding. Then I burst out from behind the tree and hissed!

"L-look!" Miranda shouted. Her hand trembled as she pointed to me.

I was wearing a long, tattered black robe. A thick black veil covered my face. "Mortal trespassers," I moaned, walking toward them. "You have awakened me from my slumber!"

"Who are you?" Miranda demanded. "And what do you want from us?"

"I am Ida Montrose, the third headmistress in White Oak history." I reached out a black-gloved hand. "Wheeeere are your hall passssssessss?"

Everyone stepped back. But not Dana. She marched right up to me. "You guys!" Dana snorted. "Can't you see? Someone from school is under that veil playing a trick on us."

"Careful, Dana," Phoebe warned. "She might really be a ghost!"

"And you don't want to make a headmistress

mad!" I added. "Especially a *dead* headmistress!"

"I told you, Ashley," Dana snapped over her shoulder, "I'm not scared of anything!"

Dana reached for my veil. But when she yanked it off, she screamed.

"Eeeek! It's . . . it's . . . "

It was still me. But under the black veil I was wearing Cheryl's Delightful Doughnut Boy mask—the one with the powdered-sugar face, doughnut eyes, and cherry nose!

"D-D-D-Dougie!" Dana stammered. She stepped back. Then she whirled around and began to run!

"Gotcha!" I said.

"What's the matter, Dana?" Ashley called after her. "Are your *nerves of steel* having a meltdown?"

But Dana was already stumbling out of the woods.

I laughed out loud behind my mask. It was finally payback time for Ashley. And I had helped!

"What's going on here?" Jasmine demanded. "What's with the Dougie mask?"

"Show them, Mary-Kate," Ashley said.

"Mary-Kate?" Miranda gasped.

I pulled the mask off my face and grinned.

Miranda and the rest of the committee stared at me with their mouths open wide.

"Mary-Kate, I can't believe that was you!" Miranda gushed. "That performance was totally cool!"

"Thanks." I pointed to the tree where the skeleton hung. "But I did have a little help."

Everyone looked up. Campbell was high in the tree, dangling the skeleton by a string. She waved.

After Campbell climbed down, Miranda walked over to me. "Mary-Kate, will you play Ida Montrose at Hair-Raiser House this Friday night?" she asked.

I gasped. "Friday?" I asked. "But isn't Friday . . . Halloween?"

Miranda nodded. "I know we booted you out of Hair-Raiser House, Mary-Kate. But you just proved that you can scare the living daylights out of people!"

Diary, I was in total shock. All I'd wanted to do was help Ashley scare Dana—but I'd ended up scaring Miranda and the whole committee!

"Thanks," I said. "But what about Valerie Metcalf?"

"Valerie can play Queen Vampira," Miranda replied. "But Ida Montrose will be the star of Hair-Raiser House."

"The star!" Ashley squealed.

I liked the sound of that! "Great!" I said happily.

"So come on, Ida," Miranda said. "Use that lantern to get us out of here!"

I lifted the lantern and said in a deep, creepy voice, "Walk this way!"

As I led everyone out of the woods, I felt like doing cartwheels. Ashley and I had both reached our goals. She'd found a way to scare Dana. And I'd gotten into Hair-Raiser House!

And we'd done it as a *team*!

Diary, this is going to be the best Halloween ever. Bring it on!

Dear Diary,

HAPPY HALLOWEEN!

I know Halloween was yesterday. But Hair-Raiser House was such a major success that we were partying practically all night!

Tons of kids from White Oak and Harrington showed up to check out our spooky rooms. There was the Dungeon of Darkness, the Monster Maze, the Grove of Man-eating Plants, and Dracula's Disco—to name a few. But the best part was seeing Mary-Kate walk through the halls as the spooky Ida Montrose!

Everyone had a total blast. Even Mrs. Pritchard

showed up and gave Hair-Raiser House an A+!

Yeah!!!

This morning at breakfast, Mary-Kate and I had a lot to talk about. "You and Phoebe did a great job on those rooms last night," Mary-Kate told me.

"Thanks!" I pushed my breakfast tray along the counter. "And you were an awesome dead Head."

"I guess Mr. Boulderblatt thought so, too." Mary-Kate grabbed a container of milk. "He asked me to be in the school musical this spring. *Little Shop of Horrors!*"

"Go, Mary-Kate!" I cheered. I held on to my tray with one hand and high-fived her with the other.

As we neared the oatmeal bowls, Dana walked into the dining hall. She stopped to get a clean tray at the stack.

"Hey," Mary-Kate said, "do you think Dana is still mad at us for scaring her?"

"There's only one way to find out." I turned toward Dana as she walked by. "Hi, Dana. Great job as the hunchback yesterday."

"Yeah," Mary-Kate agreed. "You're a real Quasimodo."

"Thanks," Dana said. She cracked a small smile. "And thanks for something else."

"Something else?" I asked. "What?"

"For scaring me the other night," Dana declared.

"It was one of the best things that ever happened to me." Dana smiled

Mary-Kate and I looked at each other. Was she serious?

"You're joking, right?" I asked Dana.

Dana shook her head. "That whole Dougie stuff in the woods got me thinking," she explained. "It's not good to be that scared of something. So I've decided to get help."

"Wow, Dana!" I said. "You mean you're going to a guidance counselor?"

"No," Dana said. "I'm going to the supermarket. For a whole box of Delightful Doughnuts—and a free Dougie mask!" She shrugged and walked to the end of the breakfast line.

"Amazing," Mary-Kate said, shaking her head.

"We actually did Dana a favor," I said. "Do you think this means she owes us one?"

"I hope so." Mary-Kate laughed. "Maybe she'll do our laundry."

We each grabbed a bowl of oatmeal. Then we headed toward a table with our trays.

"You know what?" I said. "Hair-Raiser House was more goofy fun than scary."

"Yep," Mary-Kate agreed. "But here's something that's *really* scary!"

Now what? I stopped walking and stared at my

sister. Mary-Kate pointed to the orange and yellow triangles bobbing around in our bowls.

"Candy-corn oatmeal!" Mary-Kate said. "Be scared! Be very, very scared!"

Dear Diary,

"I want to find out how much ice skates cost," I told my friend, Summer. We were shopping in the mall for Christmas presents.

"For Mary-Kate?" Summer asked. "That's so sweet of you. Everyone knows how much Mary-Kate wants those skates."

"I don't think I'll have enough money to get them," I told Summer. I had spent most of the money my Dad had sent for holiday presents on silly things like magazines, and movies, and candy. "So don't say anything, okay?"

"Not a word." Summer promised.

Sports Mania had the Olympic Gold ice skates in Mary-Kate's size—but they cost forty dollars!

"I guess this means no skates for Mary-Kate," Summer said. "Forty dollars is a lot of money."

Especially when I have five people on my Christmas list and only twenty-five dollars to spend! I thought.

I left the store, but I couldn't stop thinking about the skates. They had gleaming silver blades and a small picture of an Olympic torch on the white leather boots.

I knew Mary-Kate had spent a lot of money on my present—the coolest leather jacket. It just wasn't fair that I couldn't give my sister the one thing she really wanted for Christmas.

If there really is a Santa Claus, I'll get the money somehow, I thought.

Okay, so that was a totally silly thought. But it's Christmas, and I was desperate!

I stopped suddenly when Summer and I reached the center of the mall. The park benches, wooden planters, and big potted trees had been moved to the edges to make room for *Santa's Station.*

"Wow!" Summer and I both stared. Several huge

Christmas trees were covered in fake snow, white lights, gold bows, and red decorations. Plastic reindeer, elves, and giant candy canes stood on mounds of cotton around a red sleigh. The sleigh was piled with presents.

Santa Claus sat on a golden throne. Mrs. Claus stepped out of a small building that had been decorated to look like a gingerbread house.

The Santa scene was fantastic, but that's not what caught my eye. I stared at a sign by the rope gate.

SANTA GIRL WANTED

Maybe Santa Claus is coming to my rescue! I thought. I didn't know exactly what a Santa Girl was, but it didn't really matter. If Santa was paying money, then this was the job for me. Then I'd be able to buy all my presents.

"I'm hungry," Summer said. "Let's get a snack at the Cookie Cutter."

"You go on," I said. "I'll meet you there in a minute." I was afraid to tell Summer that I was going to try to be a Santa Girl.

I had never applied for a job before. If Santa turned me down, I didn't want any one to see.

Mrs. Claus had rosy cheeks and curly white hair.

She wore a ruffled cap, candy-striped blouse, and ruffled white apron. The pointed toes on her green shoes curved up.

I took a deep breath and walked over to her.

Mrs. Claus took a picture of a little boy sitting on Santa's lap. Then she smiled at me. "Can I help you?"

I was so nervous I blurted out the words. "I want the Santa Girl job."

"Oh, my," Mrs. Claus said. "How old are you?"

"Twelve," I said. "I'm a really good worker."

"That's younger than I had wanted," Mrs. Claus said.

No job, no money, no skates for Mary-Kate.

I have to win Mrs. Claus over, Diary. I just have to!

Dear Diary,

After class today, I sat on the floor in my room surrounded by paper, bows, and tags. I'm not very good at wrapping presents, but I love doing it anyway. Getting ready for Christmas is almost as much fun as Christmas day.

When the phone rang, I was sure it was Ashley. She really wants to be a Santa's helper at the mall. Personally, *nothing* could get me to wear a Christmas costume with green elf shoes and white tights!

But the caller wasn't Ashley. It was Great-aunt Morgan.

"Hi!" I said. "Your Christmas package came Saturday. Ashley just loves the red mittens. She really needed new ones."

"I'm happy to hear that!" Great-aunt Morgan sounded pleased. "Does the vest fit you all right?"

"It's a perfect fit!" *And that's the truth,* I thought with relief. I don't like lying, not even to be kind. "You knitted it, right?"

"Yes, I did. I designed the vest, too," Great-aunt Morgan said.

"Really? It's very-unusual," I said. I didn't know what else to say about the ugly black vest with the yellow buttons and yellow-and-green pompom trim. "Ashley and I took pictures of each other wearing the mittens and vest to send you."

"You didn't have to do that," Great-aunt Morgan said. "You and Ashley can wear them when I take you out to lunch a week from Friday."

"Lunch?" I spoke too loud, but I was surprised. "Where?"

"Wherever you girls want to go," Great-aunt Morgan said. "I'll be at White Oak at noon to pick you up."

This can't be happening! I thought in a panic. *I don't* have *the vest!*

"Great," I said, but I felt numb when I hung up. I had given the vest to my friend Summer. She had surprised me with a cool baseball jersey for Christmas, and the vest was all I had. I know that passing on unwanted gifts is a terrible thing to do to a friend.

But now, Diary, I need to get that vest back—quick!

Win a **mary-kateandashley** back-to-school kit!

Enter below to win your very own backpack from the mary-kateandashley brand

5 LUCKY WINNERS

Plus these FUN school supplies:

- *Notebooks*
- *Stationery*
- *A journal*
- *Memo board with a dry erase pen*
- *Gel pens*
- *Pens*
- *Magnetic photo frame*

mary-kateandashley

TWO OF A KIND™
Back-To-School Sweepstakes
OFFICIAL RULES:

1. No purchase necessary.

2. To enter complete the official entry form or hand print your name, address, age, and phone number along with the words "TWO OF A KIND Back-to-School Kit Sweepstakes" on a 3"x5" card and mail to: TWO OF A KIND Back-to-School Kit Sweepstakes, c/o HarperEntertainment, Attn: Children's Marketing Department, 10 East 53rd Street, New York, NY 10022. Entries must be received no later than **November 30, 2003.** Enter as often as you wish, but each entry must be mailed separately. One entry per envelope. Partially completed, illegible, or mechanically reproduced entries will not be accepted. Sponsors are not responsible for lost, late, mutilated, illegible, stolen, postage due, incomplete or misdirected entries. All entries become the property of Dualstar Entertainment Group, LLC, and will not be returned.

3. Sweepstakes open to all legal residents of the United States, (excluding Colorado and Rhode Island), who are between the ages of five and fifteen on November 30, 2003, excluding employees and immediate family members of HarperCollins Publishers, Inc., ("HarperCollins"), Warner Bros.Television ("Warner"), Parachute Properties and Parachute Press, Inc., and their respective subsidiaries and affiliates, officers, directors, shareholders, employees, agents, attorneys, and other representatives (individually and collectively, "Parachute"), Dualstar Entertainment Group, LLC, and its subsidiaries and affiliates, officers, directors, shareholders, employees, agents, attorneys and other representatives (individually and collectively, "Dualstar"), and their respective parent companies, affiliates, subsidiaries, advertising, promotion and fulfillment agencies, and the persons with whom each of the above are domiciled. Offer void where prohibited or restricted by law.

4. Odds of winning depend on the total number of entries received. Approximately 250,000 sweepstakes announcements published. All prizes will be awarded. Winners will be randomly drawn on or about December 15, 2003, by HarperCollins, whose decisions are final. Potential winners will be notified by mail and will be required to sign and return an affidavit of eligibility and release of liability within 14 days of notification. Prizes won by minors will be awarded to parent or legal guardian who must sign and return all required legal documents. By acceptance of their prize, winners consent to the use of their names, photographs, likeness, and biographical information by HarperCollins, Parachute, Dualstar and for publicity purposes without further compensation except where prohibited.

5. Five (5) **Grand Prize Winners** win a Back-to-School Kit, which consists of a backpack from *the mary-kateandashley* brand, notebooks, stationery, journal, memo board with a dry erase pen, gel pens, pens and magnetic photo frame. Approximate retail value of each prize is $60.00.

6. All prizes will be awarded. Only one prize will be awarded per individual, family or household. Prizes are non-transferable and cannot be sold or redeemed for cash. No cash substitute is available. Any federal, state or local taxes are the responsibility of the winner. Sponsor may substitute prize of equal or greater value, if necessary, due to availability.

7. Additional terms: By participating, entrants agree a) to the official rules and decisions of the judges, which will be final in all respects; and to waive any claim to ambiguity of the official rules and b) to release, discharge and hold harmless HarperCollins, Warner, Parachute, Dualstar, and their respective parent companies, affiliates, subsidiaries, and advertising, promotion and fulfillment agencies, from and against any and all liability or damages associated with acceptance, use or misuse of any prize received in this Sweepstakes.

8. Any dispute arising from this Sweepstakes will be determined according to the laws of the State of New York, without reference to its conflict of law principles, and the entrants consent to the personal jurisdiction of the State and Federal courts located in New York County and agree that such courts have exclusive jurisdiction over all such disputes.

9. To obtain the name of the winners, please send your request and a self-addressed stamped envelope (residents of Vermont may omit return postage) to TWO OF A KIND Back-to-School Kit Sweepstakes Winners, c/o HarperEntertainment, 10 East 53rd Street, New York, NY 10022 by January 1, 2004. Sweepstakes Sponsor: HarperCollins Publishers, Inc.

Mary-Kate
as Misty

Ashley
as Amber

Let's go
save the world...
again!

MARY-KATE AND ASHLEY
in ACTION!

only on

TOON Disney
CHANNEL

DUALSTAR ANIMATION
©2003 Dualstar Entertainment Group, LLC

Call your cable operator
or satellite provider
to request Toon Disney.

ToonDisney.com ©Disney

mary-kateandashley

GREAT
HAIRSTYLES
ARE AS
EASY AS...

① CURL IT!

② STRAIGHTEN IT!

③ CRIMP IT!

SO MANY LOOKS
TO CHOOSE FROM!

CURL & STYLE
Fashion Dolls

Real Dolls for Real Girls

With the new Mary-Kate and Ashley
Curl & Style fashion dolls, you can
create the same cool hairstyles
you see them wear in their
TV series' and movies!

So many looks to
choose from with hair
accessories and an
additional fashion!

DUALSTAR ENTERTAINMENT GROUP

mary-kateandashley.com
America Online Keyword: mary-kateandashley

MATTEL